KU-664-678

The Breadwitch
Jenny Nimmo

Illustrated by
BEN CORT

HEINEMA

0048669107

ACC. NO.		FUND
486691		JF1
LOC	CATEGORY	PRICE
ET	JSL	£3.99
20 IAN 1994		
CLASS No.		
- 823.910834 NIM		
OXFORD ES		
UNIVERSITY ARY		

First published in Great Britain 1993
by William Heinemann Ltd
an imprint of Reed Consumer Books Ltd
Michelin House
81 Fulham Road
London SW3 6RB

AUCKLAND · MELBOURNE · SINGAPORE · TORONTO

Text copyright © Jenny Nimmo 1993
Illustrations copyright © Ben Cort 1993
ISBN 0 434 96355 0

Printed in Italy by Olivotto

A school pack of BANANA BOOKS 55–60 is
available from Heinemann Educational Books
ISBN 0 435 00109 4

Chapter One

PETER EATWELL ALWAYS believed that witches were old ladies with pointed hats and black cloaks, and of course he thought that they were wicked, but he changed his mind on the day he poured spaghetti over his sister's head.

Belinda was three, and she was a faddy eater. If she didn't like her meal she would prod it and throw it about and scream at it.

Peter had twin brothers called Rob and Roy, and a dog called Wolfgang. All the boys loved eating, but watching Belinda gave them stomach ache. It probably gave Wolfgang stomach ache too.

Mrs Eatwell tried to bribe Belinda with promises of chocolates and new toys. Mr Eatwell shouted and threatened her. None of it made any difference. Mealtimes were horrible. And then one day Peter took matters into his own hands. They were all enjoying Mrs Eatwell's delicious spaghetti while Belinda made shadow patterns with her fork. She held it high over her head like someone conducting an orchestra.

'Eat up, Belinda,' said Mrs Eatwell, trying to keep calm.

'Look,' said Belinda.

'She's made a shadow spider,' giggled Rob.

'Belinda, eat your spaghetti,' said Mr Eatwell in an edgy way.

'No!' said Belinda. 'No no no no NO!' She finished with an awful screech.

Mr Eatwell looked as though he were going to explode, so just to shut Belinda up, Peter poured her spaghetti over her head. It worked for a second, and then Belinda roared.

The twins shrieked with laughter,
their mother screamed and their father
jumped out of his seat.

Peter ran out of the house. He was
afraid of Mr Eatwell's angry purple face.

'Peter, come back this minute!' called
Mrs Eatwell. 'Where do you think
you're going?'

But Peter didn't know. Help! he cried
inside himself. We need help. He ran to
the corner shop and looked at the
advertisements in the window. There
were so many things for sale, so many
things wanted: bicycles, kittens, beds,
carpets, babysitters . . .

I'll never find the kind of help we
need, he thought.

And then, as though a wish had been
granted, he saw exactly what he
wanted; a small card tucked into the
corner of the window. The writing was
very beautiful and it glimmered
slightly. It read:

B·T·BREADWITCH
Delectable dishes at reasonable prices
Appetites miraculously revived. Best
quality ingredients. Please call at
Basket Cottage, Munching Hill

Chapter Two

MUNCHING HILL RAN west beside the corner shop. It was very steep and Peter found himself striding up and up into a giant sunset. He could hardly make out the scenery around him, but there was no mistaking Basket Cottage. The thatched roof looked just like a basket turned upside down.

A delicious golden, crusty smell

drifted from the cottage. Peter sniffed and sniffed and, before he knew it, he was knocking on the little brown door.

'Come in, dear! Come in!' said a small figure wrapped in shadows. Peter followed his nose into a lamplit kitchen, which looked just like a picture in a fairy tale.

'Are you B.T. Breadwitch?' he asked, looking at a small person in a white apron.

'Indeed,' she said.

'Is it a meal you want or just a loaf?'

So Peter told her all about the mealtime battles, how Belinda wouldn't eat, and how his mum and dad were sick with worry. 'When I saw your advertisement I thought perhaps you'd be able to help, Mrs er . . .'

'Breadwitch will do,' she said with a smile. 'I know just what you need.' She turned a wheel on the wall and down came a rack with tiny round loaves perched on it. It stopped right beside Peter.

'Choose one,' said the Breadwitch. 'They're all the same. My *very special bread.*'

'Thank you!' said Peter, selecting a particularly crusty loaf. 'How much do I owe you?'

'It's free,' she told him, 'for people in

trouble. Just a warning, though, before you go. Keep it out of sight and only let Belinda eat it, or your troubles will get worse. Now off you go, and let me know how things work out. I take a great interest in all my customers.'

The Breadwitch showed Peter to the door. When he stepped outside, the sun had gone and a dark wind was rocking the trees.

'I hope you don't mind me asking,' said Peter, 'but what does B.T. stand for? Are you something to do with telephones?'

'Oh no, dear. I never use the phone,' she said. 'B is for Best and T for Terrestrial. I'm the Best Terrestrial Breadwitch, you see.'

'Best on earth, d'you mean?'

She nodded. 'After all, there are *others*!' She looked up into the twinkling sky and closed the door.

Chapter Three

PETER CHASED THE wind all the way home. Then he got a long lecture about disobedience and he was sent straight to bed. No one noticed the special bread under his tee shirt. He put it beneath his pillow. Next day he took it downstairs for tea. He knew Belinda sometimes ate toast, so he cut a slice. While his mother wasn't looking, he slid it into the

toaster. Then he hid the loaf behind a
biscuit tin.

'I smell toast!' said Belinda, peeping
round the door.

'Want some?' Peter asked casually.

'All right.' She sat down just as the
toast popped up.

'There you are.' Peter buttered the
toast for his sister.

The kettle whistled and the twins came in. All at once, the kitchen was a very busy place. Tea was poured, bread was cut, jam was spread and biscuits grabbed. Peter didn't notice that Belinda was feeding Wolfgang little crusts of toast – until Wolfgang jumped on to the table.

He had *never, ever* jumped on the table before.

Everyone stared at the dog, too astonished to speak, while he began to gobble up their food. Then Peter guessed what had happened. 'Oh no!' he said. 'It's the bread!'

'What bread?' cried Mrs Eatwell.

'The . . . the . . . magic . . . I mean . . . the special bread,' said Peter.

Mrs Eatwell spied the tiny loaf behind the biscuit tin. 'Is this the magic bread?' she asked.

'Yes,' said Peter unhappily. 'But it's not exactly magic.'

'Where did you get it?'

'A lady gave it to me.'

'Peter, I've told you never to take food from a stranger,' said his mother.

'Yes, but . . .'

'No buts, Peter,' said Mr Eatwell sternly and, before Peter could stop him he had broken up the bread and thrown it out of the window.

That night Wolfgang ate two tins of dogfood for supper and still he wasn't satisfied. He usually had Belinda's leftovers but there weren't any. She'd finished every scrap.

It works, thought Peter as he climbed the stairs to bed. But will Belinda be hungry tomorrow?

He looked out into the garden before he got undressed. The grass was covered with a fine golden frost of sparkly breadcrumbs.

Chapter Four

Next morning the birds woke Peter. He had never heard them sing so loudly. He pulled back the curtains and a row of starlings looked in at him. There were birds in every tree, all along the garden wall and even on the washing-line.

Peter ran downstairs. Rob and Roy were staring out of the kitchen window.

'Look!' they shouted. 'Birds, *everywhere.*'

Peter went into the garden. There were pigeons in the ivy, jackdaws on the chimney, sparrows in the gutter and a buzzard on the roof. Crows cackled round his feet, blackbirds flew behind him and a magpie landed on his head.

'Hungry! Hungry! Hungry!' the birds all seemed to say.

Suddenly Peter knew why. The birds had found the crumbs of magic bread, the bread that was supposed to make *Belinda* hungry.

'Help!' cried Peter, running back indoors.

'Peter, there's a magpie on your head,' his mother told him. 'Take it off at once!'

'I can't,' wailed Peter. 'It ate the magic bread and now it won't go until it's been fed.'

'Really, Peter,' grumbled Mrs Eatwell, 'be sensible.'

The magpie hopped on to the table and pecked at all their breakfasts.

'Get off!' squealed Belinda. 'That's *my* bacon and I'm hungry.' This was a very unusual thing for her to say, but no one paid any attention. They were all too worried about the magpie.

Mr Eatwell took off his jacket and threw it over the bird, then he carried it into the garden. It was very cross. 'Hungry! Hungry! Hungry!' it cried as it flapped away from him.

When he got back, Wolfgang was sitting in his chair eating his sausages.

'What's happening?' moaned Mr Eatwell. 'Why is everything so hungry

today?'

Peter didn't try to explain again.

When his father went down the front path the birds followed him.

'I'm not going to school,' said Rob.

'Nor am I,' said Roy. 'The birds might go with us and everyone would laugh.'

'Don't be silly, twins,' said Mrs Eatwell. 'No treats on Saturday if you don't go to school.'

'We can't,' wailed Rob and Roy. *I must do something,* thought their mother.

After breakfast Peter ran to the shed to get his bike. Pigeons flapped, sparrows fluttered, crows cawed and the eager magpie settled on his head again.

'Get off! Get off!' cried Peter.

'Hungry! Hungry! Hungry!' the birds all squawked. When Peter jumped on his bike, the magpie sat on the handlebars and stared at him with greedy, beady eyes.

'You've forgotten your schoolbooks!' called Mrs Eatwell as Peter rode away.

'I'll be back,' he said. He wasn't going to school yet!

Chapter Five

Munching Hill was so steep, Peter had
to push his bike all the way to the top.
When he reached Basket Cottage, the
bright daylight showed him things he'd
never noticed before. How the thatch
was plaited in different shades of gold.
How the windows were like mirrors,
bouncing his reflection back at him in
startling colours. How the little door

was patterned with carved fruit and the knocker shaped just like a spoon.

Peter parked his bike beside the step and knocked. The Breadwitch opened her door almost immediately. When she saw the greedy magpie sitting on Peter's bike she seemed to know, at once, what had happened.

'Burning buns!' she said. 'Jugs of juice and ferocious flavours! The birds have had my bread.'

'Yes, they have,' said Peter. 'What can we do?'

'Feed them,' the Breadwitch told him. 'We need some different bread to take their appetites away.'

Before Peter could say a word she'd turned around and pushed out a big shining bicycle. Above the front wheel, golden loaves steamed and crackled in the biggest wicker basket he had ever seen.

'Come on, Peter,' said the Breadwitch, 'after me!' She leapt on her bike and went sailing down the hill with her wide, white apron flapping like crazy wings.

But when they reached Peter's house, something else had happened. Seven hungry cats were prowling round the garden. Rob, Roy and Belinda were watching them from the window. The birds looked down from window-sills and trees. The cats looked up with wicked grins and licked their lips. One began to climb the ivy, another climbed a tree.

'Merciful muffins!' the Breadwitch cried. 'The cats have had it too. This bread won't do the trick, I'll have to fetch some special catmint cake.' She covered the bread with her apron and lifted the basket down. 'I'll be back soon,' she said, jumping on her bicycle and disappearing quickly down the road.

Peter pushed the giant basket of bread inside the house and shut the door tightly behind him.

'Who was that?' asked Rob and Roy, leaping down the stairs. 'Who was that tiny woman with golden hair and a snowy apron?'

'That was the Breadwitch,' Peter whispered.

His mum looked out of the kitchen door. 'Peter, you should be at school,' she said. 'And what is that?'

'It's a present from . . . a friend.

She's just gone to get some catmint cake
to feed the cats.'

'What friend?' his mother asked
suspiciously. 'I've told you, Peter, never
to take . . .'

'It's all right, Mum, I *promise* you!
This bread is just for the birds.'

'Well, if you're sure,' said Mrs
Eatwell a bit uneasily, and she went
back to her cooking.

When it was time for lunch, Belinda got there first and ate two whole eggs before anyone else had started.

She'd *never, ever* done that before.

It really works, thought Peter. One slice of special toast and Belinda's got an appetite, a *huge* one.

But his problems weren't over. When Mr Eatwell came home he could hardly get to the front door. The seven cats had multiplied. Others had heard about the food in the garden and now there were too many cats to count. They howled all round the house and growled like wild animals.

Where was the Breadwitch with the catmint cake? Would she come before cats filled their garden like an army. Peter began to wonder if the Breadwitch was a dream. He remembered having a picnic, once, on Munching Hill, in a little wood at the top. There wasn't a single house in sight then, and certainly not a cottage with a golden thatch. And yet, there was the giant bread basket sitting in the hall, with the snowy apron hanging right beside it.

As daylight faded, the cats grew more desperate. They pressed their noses to the windows and stared in, hungrily.

They licked the panes and scratched the frames; their eyes glimmered a ghostly green and their beating tails made a noise like thunder. The Eatwells closed their curtains, but the row was so upsetting it put them off their supper. Only Belinda ate her meal. The rest of the family gave their food to Wolfgang who still hadn't lost his mighty appetite.

'Well, at least Belinda's had a bite,' said Mrs Eatwell. 'The world's turned upside down, it seems. We can't eat and she can't stop.'

'I told you, but you wouldn't listen,' said Peter. 'It's the special bread. First Belinda ate it and then Wolfgang. Dad threw the rest in the garden – enough to feed a hundred birds and all the cats in town. It's made them hungry, just like Belinda. The Breadwitch said no one

else must eat it.'

'Peter, dear,' said Mrs Eatwell, 'there's no such thing as a Breadwitch, and no special bread that makes you hungry. Belinda has changed her mind, that's all.'

'She doesn't want spaghetti on her head,' said Mr Eatwell. 'That cured her.'

Peter gave up. He went to watch television with his brothers, but they couldn't hear a word. The cats made so much noise; their miaowing had risen to a furious wail, like a fire-engine.

'We might as well be living in the jungle,' Mrs Eatwell shouted. She ran through the house, closing every window, but she wasn't brave enough to touch the letter-box where a paw, edged with tiny daggers, groped wildly at her.

'They'll climb down the chimney like the Big Bad Wolf!' cried Rob.

'And then they'll eat us!' yelled Roy.

'Cats don't eat people,' Mr Eatwell told them, but he didn't look too sure.

Peter began to lose heart. The Breadwitch was a trickster. She'd deserted them and soon the spell-bound cats would break into the house. What good would eating do Belinda, if she in turn were to be eaten?

Chapter Six

As PETER AND his brothers got ready for
a sleepless night, they heard a mighty
'whoosh', as though a heavy cloud had
tumbled off their house. The silence
that followed was so mysterious they
found they couldn't even whisper in it.
They peeped through the curtains and
there, on the shadowy lawn, was the
tiny woman with golden hair. She was

feeding the cats from a big round cake.
Already some lay sprawled on the grass,
smiling between their paws, their eyes
closed fast, their stomachs round and
full.

Peter ran downstairs. He took the
white apron from its hook and opened
the front door.

'Breadwitch!' he called. 'Where have
you been? You forgot your apron.'

'I'm sorry I'm late, dear,' she said. 'I had so many calls to make. You didn't think I'd forgotten you, I hope.'

'Just a bit,' admitted Peter. 'I thought I'd met you in a dream.'

'But here I am,' she said, 'every bit as real as you. I've fed the cats enough to keep them quiet for hours. When they wake up they won't bother you again. While they're asleep, it's safe to feed the birds. There's just a few minutes left before dark.'

Peter pushed the heavy basket out and together he and the Breadwitch crumbled the bread and scattered it on the lawn. The air was filled with the hum and clatter of feathers as a cloud of birds swept down from the roof, the trees and the telegraph wires.

When all the bread had gone and the birds had flown away, the Breadwitch handed Peter a small slip of paper. 'It's my recipe for Special Bread,' she said.

'But I've left out just one small ingredient. I never write it down in case it gets into the wrong hands. You see it's my secret for making people hungry.' And she whispered something into Peter's ear that made him look amazed.

'So that's what it is,' he said.

'Ssh! Never tell!' The Breadwitch put a finger to her lips. 'And only use it in an emergency.'

'I promise,' Peter said.

'And now I must fly.' She tied her apron strings and put her basket in its place. 'I've so much work to do.'

'You work at night?' asked Peter.

'Twenty-four hours and beyond,' she told him with a smile, then she hopped astride her gleaming bicycle. 'Good-bye, Peter! Happy eating!'

'Good-bye and thank you,' Peter called as she pedalled into the dark. Then he raced upstairs to get one last glimpse of her.

'What are you doing?' asked the twins.

'I'm waving good-bye to a friend,' he said.

They crawled on to the bed beside him; Belinda and Wolfgang came bouncing up too. And they all watched, through the window, as a tiny woman on a big-wheeled bicycle, sailed over the horizon. Her golden hair was flying free and shining in the moonlight.

'B.G.,' Peter murmured. 'I'd call her B.G. Breadwitch!'

'What's B.G.?' asked Belinda.

'Best Galactic,' Peter told her. 'That's the Best Breadwitch in the Galaxy.'

'Good-bye, Breadwitch,' said Belinda. 'And now I think I want some more supper!'